The Prince and the Pauper

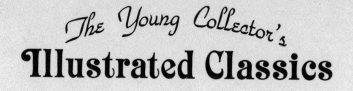

The Young Collector's
Illustrated Classics

The Prince and the Pauper

By
Mark Twain

Adapted by
Kathleen Costick

Contents

Chapter

At the Palace Gates

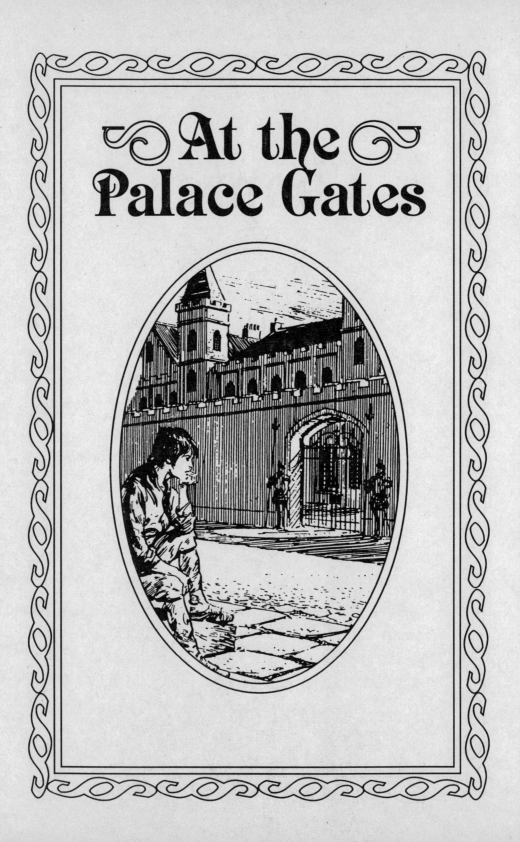

In the city of London, on a certain October day more than four hundred years ago, a boy was born to a poor family who *did not* want him.

On the same day, another English child was born to a rich family. All of England wanted this child, because he was a prince. In fact, the people of England were so glad when the prince came that they took a holiday and danced and sang for days on end. Flags waved from every housetop, and splendid parades marched through the streets.

There was no other talk in all of England except of the King's new son,

named Edward, the Prince of Wales. The little prince lay wrapped in silks and satins in a great castle; he was cared for by rich lords and ladies. But there was no talk about the other baby, Tom Canty, who lay wrapped in rags.

The streets of London were narrow,

crooked, and dirty, especially where Tom Canty grew up. His house was old and small. His whole family lived in one room. Tom and his two sisters slept on the floor in piles of dirty straw. Tom's mother and sisters were good and kind, but his father, John Canty, was a bully and a thief. He made the children beg, but he couldn't make them steal.

Tom would soon be used to being beaten by his father and to being dirty and hungry. But even so, he was not unhappy. He had a hard life, but he didn't know it. It was really no different from that of the other boys he met. When he came home with nothing, he knew his father would be angry and beat him; and he knew that, whenever she could, his mother would slip him a crust of bread.

Father Andrew, a kind, old priest, lived in another part of the same house. He taught the children how to be fair and honest. He also taught Tom some Latin and how to read and write.

Tom listened to many tales Father Andrew told about enchanted castles,

splendid kings, and princes. His head became full of such wonders. Many a night as he lay in his bed of dirty straw, he would imagine himself to be a prince. When he pictured himself in a palace surrounded by fine things, he forgot the misery around him. He became haunted by one wish—to see a real prince!

Tom daydreamed about princes and kings as he walked along the city streets. One day he was surprised to find he had wandered all the way to the edge of the

city. He had never been so far from home before. In the distance he could see the palaces of rich nobles overlooking the river. Tom rested for a few minutes by a carved stone. Then he continued down the road toward the grandest and most mighty palace of all.

Tom stared in wonder at the thick stone walls, the towers, the huge doorway covered with golden lions. Here, indeed, was a king's palace! Might he not see a real prince now? At each side of the golden gate to the palace stood a guard. They stood so straight and still; they seemed more like statues than men.

Feeling even more ragged next to so much splendor, Tom walked slowly up to the gate. His heart pounded within his chest as he approached the guards.

All at once, he caught sight of someone who almost made him want to shout for joy. He saw a boy clothed in bright silks and satins being waited on by fine-looking gentlemen—his servants, no doubt. The boy sparkled as he moved; fine jewels decorated his clothing. He was a prince—a real prince!

Tom leaned forward eagerly. He put his face to the bars of the gate. The next instant, he was grabbed by one of the guards. Shocked and frightened, Tom let

out a scream. The guard shook him and then threw him into the dusty road.

"Mind your manners, beggar!" he growled.

Hearing the commotion, the Prince turned just in time to see the poor boy thrown to the ground. The guard was standing over the beggar, scowling down at him.

The Prince sprang to the gate. His eyes flashed at the guard who had grabbed Tom so rudely.

"How dare you treat a poor lad so harshly! I should have you punished for such abuse. Now, open the gates and let him in!"

The guards opened the gates and stood silently at attention as Tom, the "Prince of Rags," passed in and joined hands with the "Prince of Never-Ending Riches."

Tom didn't know what to say. He couldn't believe he was being greeted by royalty.

Prince Edward said, "You look very

tired and hungry, lad. Come with me, and I'll get you something to eat."

The finely dressed servants of the Prince rushed forward, but the Prince waved them aside. They stopped still where they were—frozen like statues.

The Prince took Tom into a richly decorated room in the palace. Then, at his command, the servants brought a meal for Tom.

Tom had never seen such a meal before! There were three kinds of meats and countless fruits and sweets. The Prince then sent the servants away so that their staring eyes would not make Tom uncomfortable.

"What is your name, lad?" the Prince asked.

"Please sir, I am called Tom Canty, sir."

"Where do you live?" asked the Prince.

"Please sir, in the city, sir," replied Tom.

"Do you have parents?" asked the Prince.

"Yes sir, and twin sisters named Nan and Bet, sir, who are fifteen," answered Tom.

"I also have two older sisters," said the Prince, "and I have a cousin who is my age. My sister, the Princess Mary, is always gloomy and frowning. But the Princess Elizabeth and my cousin, the Lady Jane Grey, are very pretty and learn their lessons quickly. Tell me, Tom Canty, do you learn your lessons quickly?"

"I don't know, sir. The good priest, Father Andrew, teaches me out of kindness."

"Do you have a good life?" asked the Prince.

"Truly sir, I do—except when I am hungry or cold. We boys wrestle each other in the streets and race to see which one of us is the fastest," said Tom.

The Prince's eyes flashed.

"I would like to do that," he said. "Tell me more."

"In summer, sir, we swim in the river," said Tom. "We dive and shout and splash each other with water, and . . ."

"Oh, say no more!" cried the Prince. "I would give almost anything to be able to dress like you just once, and go barefoot down to the river!"

"And if I could dress like you, sir, just once," Tom said wistfully.

"You'd like that, would you?" laughed the Prince as he removed his bright, satin jacket, sparkling with gems. "Then you shall have your wish! Take off your rags and put on these splendors, lad! We will change back again before any of my noble attendants come in."

Tom jumped from the table, shocked at the Prince's suggestion. How could he dare put on royal clothes? He stood there smiling, holding his satin jacket out to Tom, who was looking in wonder at the gems. Tom looked down at his own rags, then back to the Prince.

"Come now," said the Prince. "Let's have some fun. I shall be a pauper. And you shall be a prince."

Tom smiled and chuckled, slipping off his beggar's rags.

Chapter

Pauper or Prince ?

In only a few minutes, the Prince of Wales had put on Tom's ragged outfit, and the "Prince of Paupers" had put on the silks and satins of royalty. The two went and stood side by side in front of a great mirror. To their surprise, there did not seem to be any change made! They stared at each other, then at the glass, and then at each other again.

At last the puzzled Prince said, "What do you make of this?"

"Oh sir, please do not make me answer! It is not right that someone as lowly as I am should say such a thing to someone as great as you," said Tom.

"Then I will say it. You are the same height that I am; you have the same color hair, the same color eyes, and the same voice that I have!

Now that I have your clothes on and look so much like you, I understand better how you felt when the guard at the gate . . . Did he give you that bruised hand?"

"Yes sir," said Tom. "But it is nothing."

"It was a cruel and shameful thing to do!" cried the Prince angrily, stamping his

foot. "If my father, the King, only knew of it! Stay where you are until I return!"

The Prince started toward the door.

"Oh, please sir!" cried Tom in alarm. "Don't tell the King about this," he pleaded, waving his bruised hand weakly. "I would not want His Royal Highness bothered on my account! Why, I am used to beatings from my father."

"What! Beatings?" said the Prince in horror.

"Oh, yes sir!" replied Tom quickly.

The Prince folded his arms on his chest and said in a firm voice, "Before darkness falls tonight, I will have your father put in the Tower!"

"But sir, my father is a pauper! The prison in the Tower is only for the rich!" cried Tom.

"Mmm, you are right," agreed the Prince. "I had not thought of that. I will think of another punishment for him later. Don't worry, I am not going to tell the King. I will take care of the guard who treated you so badly myself! Stay here

until I return. And remember, that is a command!"

Again the Prince turned to leave, but seeing that he had left something of great importance lying on a table, he stopped. Hastily, he picked up an object that had a handle. He then hid it in a place where only he would know to find it.

The next moment, he was out the door, flying across the palace grounds in his tattered rags. His face was pink with

The Prince and the Pauper

anger; and his eyes glowed. As soon as he reached the gateway, he seized the bars and shouted to the guards.

"Open these gates this instant!"

The guard who had thrown Tom into the street rushed forward to open the gates and, as the Prince ran out, he slapped him soundly on the ear. The startled Prince was hurled into the mud.

The guard growled, "Take that, beggar, for getting me into trouble with the Prince!"

A small crowd of onlookers gathered to see what the fuss was about and laughed at the sight of the ragged boy splattered with mud. They clapped their hands and cheered the guard.

The Prince picked himself up and shook his fist at the guard, crying fiercely, "I am the Prince of Wales! My father is the King of England! You will hang for having dared to lay a hand on me!"

The guard brought his long spear up to his face and pretended to salute the Prince.

"I salute Your Royal Highness," he mocked. Then he shouted angrily, "Take yourself away from here, beggar boy, before I throw you away!"

More and more people gathered at the palace gates. They made fun of the poor

boy who kept saying over and over again that he was Edward, Prince of Wales. They were very amused by his bold display of temper. Finally, the crowd closed in around him, pushing him down the street.

"Make way for His Royal Highness!

Make way for the Prince of Wales!" they shouted.

When he had waved his arms and protested that he was the Prince, he had been very amusing. But when he became too tired to threaten them with royal commands, the crowd soon lost interest in him. At last, they deserted him.

The Prince looked around him, but nothing he saw was familiar to him. He was *somewhere* in the city of London. He knew nothing more than that. He wan-

The Prince and the Pauper

dered on and on, growing tired and hungry.

After a while he came to a huge church. He had seen the church before.

It was a very old church, and it was being repaired. A wooden framework had been built around it to support all the people while they worked on it.

The Prince took heart at once; he felt that his troubles were at an end.

He said to himself, "This is the ancient church called Christ's Church which my father has made into a home for poor, homeless children. They will be glad to help the son of the King, who has been so good and generous to them—especially when he is poor and needy too."

Chapter

3

A Change of Homes

The Prince walked up to a crowd of boys who were playing leap-frog in front of the church. They were all dressed alike. Each wore a long, blue coat with a wide, red belt, a shirt with full sleeves, bright yellow socks, and black shoes with big, metal buckles. They stopped playing when they saw him.

The Prince called to them.

"Good lads, please run and tell your master that Edward, Prince of Wales, wants to speak to him."

A great shout went up at this. One boy cried, "Are you a messenger from the palace then, beggar?"

The boys laughed. Edward drew himself up proudly and said, "I am the Prince. You are all clothed and fed by my good father, the King. Out of regard for him, you should not laugh at me."

The boys enjoyed this speech

immensely. They howled in amusement. The first boy who had spoken shouted to the others, "Down on your knees, slaves! Where are your manners? You'd starve if the King did not pity you! Down on your knees before his son's royal rags!"

All at once the boys dropped to their knees and pretended to pay homage to the Prince. Edward was enraged.

"Don't you dare mock me or I'll see that you all swing from the gallows!" he cried fiercely.

The boys stopped laughing and stared, speechless, at the Prince. They had been playing a game with him. His threat of the gallows, however, was beyond fun. Suddenly, they all rushed up together and seized him, lifting him into the air.

"Throw him in the pond!" they shouted angrily. "Set the dogs on him!"

Then something happened that had never happened before in the long history of England—the heir to the crown was rudely beaten by commoners and chased by dogs.

As darkness fell that day, the Prince found himself in the dirtiest section of the city. His body was bruised, and his rags were covered with mud. He wandered on aimlessly. He was so tired that he could hardly walk. He had stopped trying to ask questions of anyone because that only brought him more insults.

He muttered to himself, "If only I can find Tom's family—then I will be saved!

Tom's parents will take me to the palace and prove that I am not their son but the true Prince!"

Now and then he thought of how badly he had been treated by the boys of Christ's Church.

"When I am King," he decided, "those boys will not only be clothed and fed, they will be taught too. They are rude because they are not in school."

Lights began to twinkle throughout the city. It started to rain. The wind began to blow, and a storm seemed about to break. The Prince moved on wearily. He drifted deeper and deeper into a maze of crooked, dirty alleys where the most miserable people in all London were huddled together.

Suddenly a great, drunken brute grabbed him by the collar.

"Out 'til this time of night! And I'll bet you don't have a penny to show for it!" the man said. "If you don't, then I'll break every bone in your lean body or my name isn't John Canty!"

The Prince twisted himself loose and exclaimed, "Oh, are you really his father?"

"*His* father?" said the man. "What are you talking about? I'm your father!"

"Oh, don't joke with me, please!" cried the Prince. "I am tired and wounded; I can't bear any more! Take me to my father, the King, and he will make you rich beyond your wildest dreams! Believe me, I speak the truth! I am Edward, Prince of Wales!"

The man stared down at the Prince, shook his head, and muttered, "He's gone stark-raving mad!" He grabbed the Prince again and laughed, "But mad or not, you're coming home with me!"

With this, he dragged the struggling Prince away into the darkness.

The Prince and the Pauper

All this time, Tom Canty had been left alone in Prince Edward's room. He stood in front of the mirror admiring his sparkling appearance. Then he walked away, imitating the Prince's high-born manner.

Tom examined all the beautiful things in the room. He thought of how proud he would be if his mother, sisters, and friends in the city could peek in and see him in such splendor. He wondered if they would believe him when he told them of his day in the palace. Would they shake their heads and say he had been dreaming again?

After an hour, it suddenly occurred to Tom that the Prince had been gone for a long time. He began to feel lonely and restless. Then he became worried.

Suppose someone came in and discovered him in the Prince's clothes? They might send him to the gallows at once without waiting for the Prince to return.

Tom became more and more afraid as the minutes ticked by. He decided to go

and look for the Prince. He softly opened
the great door at the end of the room. A
small crowd of gentlemen servants sprang
to their feet and bowed low before him.
Tom stepped back quickly and shut the
door.

"Oh, how they mock me!" he said to himself. "They will go and tell on me! Oh, why did I ever come here? I have thrown my life away! *Where can the Prince be?*"

Tom walked up and down the room nervously. He was so tense that he jumped at even the slightest noise from behind the great door.

At long last the door swung open and a servant came in and announced, "The Lady Jane Grey."

A young girl ran to Tom. But she stopped suddenly when she saw how distressed he was.

"Oh what is the matter, my lord?" she asked.

Tom fell down on his knees. "Have m-m-m-mercy on me, please!" he stammered. "Truly, I am not a lord, but only poor Tom

Canty! Please let me see the Prince! He will give me back my rags and let me go away unharmed!"

The young girl seemed horrified.

"Oh my lord," she cried, "on your knees—and to *me*!"

Then she turned and ran away.

"Oh no, now I am lost," moaned Tom. "Now they will come in and take me to the gallows!"

Chapter

Tom and the King

While Tom waited for the guards to rush in and take him prisoner, rumors spread through the palace. The whisper— for it was never said aloud but always whispered—flew from servant to servant, from lord to lady, from one grand room to the next.

"The Prince is mad!" they all said.

A nobleman came in and said that Tom should follow him. Tom walked slowly down the great hall. As he walked, everyone bowed low before him.

The servants all agreed that their Prince was mad.

Tom was brought to a richly decorat-

ed room where he saw a table set for one. The meal before him was even more grand than the one he had enjoyed earlier, when he had been questioned by the Prince.

Tom was very confused. The noble-man waved his hand toward the chair at the head of the table. He expected Tom to sit down and eat. Tom was so used to being hungry that—even though he was nervous and upset—he ate the food in front of him eagerly.

Tom felt strange eating with so many gentlemen staring at him. Each time he

tried to do something for himself, one of the splendid gentlemen rushed forward to do it for him. When he reached for the meat, one rushed to serve him. When he put down his cup, another rushed to fill it. It was a wonder that no one tried to eat for him.

At the end of the meal a shallow, golden dish of rosewater was placed on the table for him to wash his fingers. Tom was puzzled by the dish. Finally, he raised it to his lips and drank it!

The servants said nothing. By the time Tom had arrived at this delicious feast, the rumor of the Prince's madness had spread to the King. As a result, a special order had been issued to every person in the palace. The order was signed by King Henry VIII. It said that anyone found repeating or even listening to the foolish rumor about the Prince of Wales would be put to death immediately!

The servants looked sadly at the Prince. They could not believe their eyes. Although they could say nothing, they were all thinking the same thing: the Prince was surely mad—drinking rosewater from a finger bowl.

Having finished his meal, Tom waited for some sign as to what he was to do next. The same nobleman who had taken Tom to the dining room came to get him. He led Tom to another room in the palace—a very grand room.

Tom found himself standing in front of a man with grey whiskers, who regarded him sternly. The man seemed to have

sunk into a chair covered with cushions of the most costly fabric. One of his legs was swollen and bandaged. He appeared to be in a great deal of pain. Tom could hear his heavy breathing all the way across the room.

The man, stern as he looked, spoke in a very gentle voice to the boy before him.

"Tell me, Edward," he said. "Tell the good King, your father, what it is that troubles you."

As soon as he heard the words, "the good King," Tom dropped to his knees.

"*You* are the King!" Tom cried. "Oh, please good sir, have mercy on me!"

The King was stunned. He shook his head in disbelief and stared, wide-eyed, at Tom. Then he said in a voice heavy with disappointment.

"Alas, I thought the rumor was false. I am afraid it may be true after all."

He extended his hand to Tom.

"Come here to your father, child. You are ill."

Poor Tom trembled as he approached His Majesty. The King gazed earnestly into Tom's face.

"You feel better now, don't you Edward? You had a bad dream, didn't you?" he said.

"Oh please, Your Highness, believe me!" begged Tom. "I am really one of your poorest subjects. I am only here by mis-

take! I've done nothing wrong—please do not be angry with me!"

The King sighed and patted his cheek tenderly.

"Now child," he said, "do not be afraid. There is no one here who does not love you."

But to himself the King said, "Perhaps he is only mad about this matter, and his mind is clear on all others. I will test him."

The King paused for a moment and then asked Tom a question in Latin. Tom answered in the same language.

The King's face broke into a broad smile. The nobleman who had brought Tom to the King's chamber also seemed very relieved that he had answered well. The King turned to him and said in a deep, gruff voice,

"My son is mad, but his madness is not permanent. It results from too many long hours of study. He must relax and enjoy himself. Send his teachers away, and see that he has plenty of wholesome exercise out-of-doors. Fresh air and sunshine will clear his mind and restore his health."

Tom was so distressed to hear the King call him "Edward" and "my son" that he could not speak. He could only nod his head and hope that the real Prince would return soon and explain everything.

Tom left the King's chamber with a heavy heart. He had hoped to be set free.

Now he realized that he was a captive in a golden cage. His spirits sank lower and lower as he walked from one great room to the next, past crowds of royal attendants. They all bowed before him.

Tom's adviser brought him to the door of the Prince's room. Tom hesitated but then asked, "Would it be all right if I were alone?"

"If it pleases Your Highness. It is for you to command and for us to obey," said the nobleman.

Tom took down several pieces of shining steel armor from the walls of the Prince's chamber. He put on the helmet, the gloves, and the other pieces he could manage without help. He began to daydream in front of the mirror

He thought of the King, who had called him his son. Then he thought of what the King had said, about ruling England. The words rang in Tom's ears still.

"Listen to me, Edward," the King had said to Tom. "You are my son and

England's heir. You must rule when I am gone. For my sake—for England's sake—you must try to hide the trouble in your mind. It is like a dark cloud; it casts a terrible shadow and it frightens us, but it soon passes on. We must be patient. Promise me you will not deny you are the true Prince. If ever you are unsure of how to act or of what to say, turn to your noble adviser for help. You will be well again soon."

Tom trembled when he thought that someday he might have to rule England. What did he know of being a king? He could daydream, but he could never really be a king. Yes, he knew his Latin and had studied hard, but he had not been born to royal parents.

Tom thought of his family. He wondered how they were doing now that he wasn't there to beg for them. He wondered what they were doing at that very moment.

Chapter

A Dirty Room for the Prince

When last seen, the true Prince was being dragged down a dark alley by John Canty, Tom's nasty father. Soon, he found himself in the dirty room where the Canty family lived. By the dim light of a single candle, he saw a woman and two girls cowering in the corner.

John Canty called to them, "I've a surprise for you! Tell 'em who you are, boy!"

The Prince drew in a sharp breath.

"I tell you now as I told you before," he said. "I am Edward, Prince of Wales!"

Tom's mother and sisters stared at the Prince in amazement. Then they ran

towards him exclaiming, "Oh poor Tom, our poor boy!"

The mother fell on her knees before the Prince, put her hands upon his shoulders, and gazed lovingly into his eyes. Tears streamed down her face.

"Oh my poor boy!" she said. "Your foolish reading has taken away your wits at last! Now you have broken your mother's heart!" The Prince looked into her face and said gently, "Good woman, your son is well. He has not lost his wits. Take me to the palace where he is, and my father, the King, will bring him to you."

"Your father, the King!" cried the woman. "Oh my child, how can you say such a thing? You will bring ruin on all of us! Shake off this terrible dream, Tom. Call back your wandering memory. Look at me. Don't you know who I am? I am your mother—your mother who loves you!"

The Prince shook his head sadly and said, "I am sorry to make you unhappy, poor woman, but I have never seen your face before."

The woman sank back on the floor and, covering her face with her hands, wept aloud.

John Canty laughed.

"Let the show go on! What, Nan! What, Bet! Will you stand in the presence of the Prince of Wales? Down on your knees, both of you! Show some respect for His Royal Highness!"

Tom's sisters began to plead timidly.

"Let him go to bed, Father," Nan said.

"Rest and sleep will cure him of this strange madness."

"Yes, Father," said Bet. "He is tired. He will not come home empty-handed tomorrow."

This remark made John Canty think of money. He turned angrily to the Prince.

"Tomorrow we must pay two pennies rent to the owner of this miserable hole or we will be turned out! Show me what you have gathered with your lazy begging!"

The Prince glared at him and said, "Don't insult me with your low concerns. I tell you I am the King's son!"

A crude blow from John Canty's hand sent the Prince staggering into the arms of Tom's mother. The good woman tried to protect him from Tom's father by placing herself in front of him, taking Canty's blows herself. The Prince sprang away from Mrs. Canty and cried, "I will not let you suffer for me, madam. I will face this bully alone."

This speech angered John Canty so much that he beat the boy soundly; then

he struck the mother and the two girls for having showed pity for him.

"Now, go to bed, all of you", he said gruffly, after he had finished.

As soon as they heard John Canty snoring, the girls crept to where the Prince lay and covered him tenderly with straw and rags. Their mother crept to him also. She stroked his hair and whispered words

of comfort in his ear. She gave him something to eat, too, but the Prince was not hungry—at least not for dry, tasteless crusts of bread.

The Prince was very touched by her brave attempts to defend him, and he thanked her in noble words. He added that his father, the King, would be sure to reward her for her kindness.

As Tom's mother lay in her bed of straw, an idea came into her mind. She tried not to pay any attention to it, but she found she could not sleep because of it. She began to wonder if the boy who lay across from her in the dark was not her son after all. She thought she saw something "different" in him, something she had never seen in Tom Canty. She didn't know what it was, but she felt it was there.

"Oh, that is silly," she thought. "He *must* be my son!" And she almost smiled, in spite of all her troubles.

But, nevertheless, the idea continued to haunt her thoughts.

Chapter

A Trusty Friend

Early the next morning, while the Canty family slept, the ragged, but real Prince escaped from the dirty hovel where they lived. He followed the river to the edge of the city and soon made his way to the palace gates. There, he steadfastly proclaimed himself to be the Prince of Wales and demanded admission to the palace.

A crowd soon collected around him, bending their necks to see the "little madman." After a while, they began to mock him. They hoped to entertain themselves by watching his fury. Tears sprang to the Prince's eyes, but he stood his ground.

"I tell you now as I told you before, I

am the Prince of Wales!" he exclaimed. "No matter how friendless and forlorn I may be, I will not be driven away!"

Suddenly, a strong voice in the crowd hailed the Prince.

"Whether you are a prince or not, you are a brave and gallant lad! And you are not friendless either. You have Miles Hendon by your side!"

A tall, well-built man pushed his way to the front of the crowd. His clothes were of a rich material but faded and threadbare. A long sword hung by his side. His speech was received with an explosion of shouts and laughter from the crowd.

"Here is another Prince in disguise!" some cried.

"Grab the boy! Throw him in the pond," said others.

Quickly, a hand was laid upon the Prince. Just as quickly, Hendon drew his sword and hurled to the ground the man who was threatening the boy.

The next moment, twenty voices shouted, "Kill the dog! Kill him! Kill him!"

The mob closed in around Hendon. He backed himself against a wall and began flinging his sword forcefully. He fought with courage. His opponents lay

sprawled this way and that, but the mob continued to rush upon him. His moments seemed numbered, and his destruction certain.

Suddenly, a trumpet blast sounded and a voice shouted, "Make way for the King's messenger!"

Horsemen came charging down upon the mob of people, who fled as fast as their legs could carry them. Miles Hendon swept the Prince up in his arms and carried him out of harm's way. He headed through back alleys toward the river and didn't stop until he was within sight of London Bridge.

The royal messengers had tremendous news for the people of England.

"The King is dead! The King is dead!" they said.

The city rang with the sad news. Hendon and the Prince heard it from a

hundred voices at once as they made their way through the crowds on London Bridge. The news struck a chill in the heart of the poor Prince and sent a shudder through his ragged frame. The King had always been kind and gentle to Edward. Tears filled the boy's eyes, and he was overcome with sadness. He felt like an outcast—but then another, more far-reaching cry thundered through the air.

"Long live King Edward VI!"

"Ah," he thought, "how strange it seems. *I am King!*"

Hendon's lodgings were in a small inn on the bridge. As they neared the door, a gruff voice behind them said, "So, there you are! After I pound your bones into pudding you'll know not to run away from me again!"

It was John Canty! He put out his hand to seize the boy, but Miles Hendon blocked the way.

"Not so fast. You're a little rough, aren't you? Who is this boy to you?" he said.

"If it's any of your business to meddle in my affairs, he is my son," snarled Canty.

"That's a lie!" cried the new King.

"Why, you little . . ." growled Canty. He reached over to grab the boy but was stopped by Hendon's sword.

"I believe you, my boy," said Hendon. "But it doesn't matter. Whether this brute is your father or not, he will not have you to beat and abuse anymore—not if you prefer to stay with me."

"I do, I do," cried the King eagerly.

"Listen you!" Hendon said, prodding Canty with the point of his sword. "I took this lad under my protection when a mob of brutes like you would have mistreated him. Do you think I would desert him now to a worse fate in your hands? So be on your way, and be quick about it."

John Canty left muttering threats.

Hendon took the young King up to his rooms and ordered a meal to be sent to them. The King dragged himself to the bed

and lay down exhausted. He murmured drowsily, "Please call me when dinner is served."

A smile twinkled in Hendon's eye as he thought, "He calls himself the Prince of Wales. Look how bravely he plays the part! He takes over my bed without so much as a 'please,' or a 'thank you.' He has been mistreated, and his troubled mind is the result of it. But I will take good care of him, and he will be cured of this sickness."

Chapter

7

King Tom and Pauper Edward

While the real Prince stood shouting and waving his arms outside the palace gates, Tom Canty was being solemnly dressed in his royal robes. It was late afternoon, but the vast riverfront of the palace was blazing with light. For as far as the eye could see, the water was crowded with gently swaying boats, all lit with bright-colored lanterns. The royal barge was to take Tom into the city. The Prince of Wales—or rather, Tom Canty—would be greeted in a great hall by the mayor of London.

As the royal barge swept along the river, the people on the shore cheered for

the Prince. Tom looked out on a glorious sight, but he was far too frightened to enjoy it. He was not the Prince. Where was Edward? He had never felt so alone.

Later, inside the hall, Tom found himself on a huge platform in front of a crowd. But as the mayor started toward him, he was stopped short by a loud trumpet blast.

One of the messengers who had charged past Edward at the gate appeared at the door and shouted, "The King is dead!"

For a moment, the people bowed their heads in silent respect for the dead king. Then, the same messenger cried, "Long live the King!"

The people looked up and held out their arms to the frightened boy in front of them. The hall shook with their mighty cheers for him.

Tom sat on a golden throne and said the words his adviser told him to say. He *looked* like a king, but he did not *feel* like a king.

The next morning, in the early hours before dawn, Tom Canty stirred out of a heavy sleep and opened his eyes in the dark. Suddenly he burst out,

"I am awake at last! Hey, Nan! Bet! Kick off your straw and come hear the wildest dream that ever the night did invent!"

A dim form appeared by his side. A voice said, "Did you call, Your Majesty?"

Tom sighed and buried his head in his pillow, feeling very homesick. He used to dream of being a king. Now that he was a king, he dreamed of being home again!

Early that same day, Hendon left his lodgings in order to buy a second-hand suit of clothes for his new friend. He

closed the door quietly behind him so he would not wake the sleeping boy.

Hendon returned shortly afterwards to find the boy gone. He was told by the owner of the inn that a strange young man had come and taken the boy away with him. Hendon ran out at once.

The strange, young man had led the King to a deserted barn in the country where he found himself face to face with John Canty! Canty locked the King in the barn. Edward sat and thought of Hendon

searching for him everywhere in London.

The King withdrew to the farthest end of the barn and was soon lost in thought. He was weary with grief for his father. And troubled, too, to realize that Hendon

would think he had deserted him. As the afternoon passed, the King dozed.

He woke to a grim sight. A bright fire was burning in the middle of the floor, and around it sprawled a group of tattered beggars and thieves.

There were men of all sizes, clothed carelessly in rags. There were blind beggars with patched eyes, and cripples with wooden legs. All of them were loud, filthy, and foul-mouthed.

The King saw one of the "blind" men get up and throw aside the patches that covered his two, good eyes. Then one "cripple" removed his wooden leg and stood up on healthy limbs.

"What brings you back to our gang, John Canty?" called the former "cripple."

"I must run from the law," replied Canty. "I struck a man on the head in a fight and killed him."

"And you shall hang for it! I will command it!" cried the King. The gang was surprised to see him walk into the firelight.

"Who is this? Who are you, boy?" they all asked.

"He is my son—a dreamer, a fool, a madman. He thinks he is the King. You'll turn me in, will you boy? Just wait until I get my hands on you," growled Canty.

"I am not your son!" cried the boy. "I am Edward, King of England!"

A wild burst of laughter followed, and a big strong "cripple" stepped in front of the King and knocked John Canty down. He smiled and said, "Have you no respect for 'kings,' Canty? Insult him again and I'll hang you myself!"

Then he turned to His Majesty with a serious look.

"Listen, boy," he said. "Be a king in your head if you want, but call yourself

another name. It is dangerous to call yourself the King of England."

A former "blind" man called out a suggestion.

"Let's call him 'Foo-Foo the First, King of the Moon'."

A roaring shout went up among them,
"Long live Foo-Foo the First, King of
the Moon!"

Almost before the poor King could say
a word, he was crowned with a tin basin,
robed in a tattered blanket, and given a
barrel for a throne. Then they all threw
themselves on their knees and wailed.

"Be good to us, O sweet King!"

"Pity your slaves, and comfort them
with a royal kick!"

Tears of shame burned in the young
King's eyes.

Chapter

Edward and the Outlaws

The gang of thieves left the barn early the next day. Their playful mood was gone, and they were all silent and glum. The sky was grey and threatened to storm. The air was very cold.

The "cripple" who had stepped between the King and John Canty the night before was the leader of the gang. He commanded Canty to stay away from the boy. The strange young man who had tricked the King into leaving Hendon's lodgings was told to look after him. His name was Hugo.

The gang was feared by all who passed them on the road. People took their

insults meekly; they didn't dare talk back. The gang snatched things from the yards of houses they passed. The owners of the houses saw them do it but said nothing.

After a while the weather became milder, and the grey clouds disappeared.

The gang grew more and more cheerful. They entered a small farmhouse and made themselves at home. They forced the trembling farmer and his wife to make breakfast for them, and insulted them while they ate. They threw carrots at the farmer's children and laughed when a hit was made.

When they left, the gang threatened to come back and burn the house down if the family reported them to the law officers in the area.

At noon, they stopped outside a large village. The "cripples" put on their wooden legs, and the "blind" men put patches and bandages over their eyes. They were going to scatter, enter the village at different places, and begin "work."

The King was told to go into the village and "work" with Hugo. Hugo was watching for a chance to steal, and the King was watching for a chance to escape.

Hugo said, "This is a poor place. I don't see anything to steal. Therefore, we will beg."

"We will beg?" replied the King. "I won't!"

"You won't beg?" exclaimed Hugo. "But your father said you begged for him! That's why he wanted to take you away from that man on the bridge, Miles

Hendon, and make you join our gang—so you could "work" for us and bring us money!"

"That brute Canty is not my father!" said the King.

"Don't play your mad tricks with me,

boy!" cried Hugo. "If you won't beg and you won't steal, you can at least pretend to cry while *I* beg!"

The King was about to refuse when Hugo said, "Hush! Here comes a man with a kind face now! I will fall down and pre-

tend to be sick. When the man runs over, you fall down on your knees and cry out to him, 'Oh sir, look at my poor brother! We have no friends and have been turned out of our house! Take pity on us and give us a penny for something to eat!' And don't stop wailing until he gives us the money!"

Then, Hugo staggered and fell down on the ground in front of the stranger.

"Oh dear!" cried the good stranger. "Let me help you!"

"Oh sir," cried Hugo pitifully, "my brother there will tell you how poor and sick I am! Please give us a penny, kind sir!"

"A penny!" replied the good man. "I will give you three!" He fumbled in his pocket for the money. "Here lad," he said, holding out his hand to the King. "Take this money. Then help me carry your poor sick brother to that inn where I . . ."

"I am not his brother," said the King.

"What! Not his brother!" stammered the man.

"Oh, listen to him!" groaned Hugo. "He would desert his own brother—and me with one foot in the grave!" Hugo looked up and glared at the King.

"Shame on you, boy!" cried the man. "He is so sick that he can hardly move. If he is not your brother, then who is he?"

"He is a beggar and a thief!" cried the King. "When you reached into your pocket

for the pennies, he stole the wallet out of your coat!"

The man slapped his coat in the place where his wallet had been and, finding it gone, raised his staff over Hugo's head. Hugo leapt to his feet and ran down the street. The man he had robbed ran after him, shouting with all his might.

The King ran in the opposite direction as fast as his legs would go. He did not stop running until he was well into the country beyond the village.

Edward felt very hungry and tired. He decided to stop at a farmhouse and ask for help; but before he could speak, he was rudely driven away. They didn't want to hear what such a ragged boy had to say.

He wandered on. As darkness fell, he made another attempt to seek help at a farmhouse and was treated even worse than before. He was called terrible names and told he would be arrested if he didn't move on.

Night came and still the King walked

slowly on. He had to keep moving; every time he sat down to rest, he turned numb with cold. The sounds he heard seemed muffled and very far away. Once in a while a light flickered in the distance. He had never felt so alone before or so far away from other people as he did in the dark, empty night. All his life he had been fol-

lowed wherever he went by crowds of loving attendants.

At last, he came to another farmhouse with a barn nearby. The door to the barn was open. The King crept inside and curled up in the straw in one of the stalls. He was about to fall asleep when he felt something touch him in the dark.

The horror of that touch almost made his heart stand still. He put out his hand slowly and felt something warm and soft. It was a calf!

The King was glad to have the calf's company. Feeling almost happy for the first time since he had become a pauper, he fell asleep. The calf slept too. It was a simple creature—not at all troubled to share his bed with a King.

Chapter

Hugo's Revenge

When the King awoke in the early morning he heard the sound of children's voices outside the barn. The door opened and two little girls came in.

As soon as they saw him, they stopped laughing and talking. They stared at him with wide eyes, as if he were some strange, new kind of animal.

One of them asked, "Who are you?"

"The King of England," he said gravely.

The children looked at him in wonder. They believed him. They began at once to question him about how he came to be in their barn, and why he was so ragged and worn. The King told them the story of his troubles. It was a great relief to be able to tell it to someone and not be laughed at. The little girls were very sorry for him.

The girls ran off to get some breakfast for the King, who thought to himself, "When I am back in my rightful place again, I will remember how these children trusted and believed me. Those who were older, and thought themselves wiser, laughed and called me a liar."

As he waited for the girls to come back, Edward looked around the clean, well-swept barn, now bright with sun-

shine. He smiled at the calf who had been his companion in the gloomy night. He now felt closer to the common people farming the land than he had ever felt before.

Just at that moment, he was jerked from his pleasant thoughts and dragged, kicking and screaming, out of the barn by John Canty and Hugo.

Once again, "King Foo-Foo the First" was roving the countryside with the gang of outlaws. He often found himself the target of their crude jokes, and they would force him to take part in their merrymaking.

None but John Canty and Hugo, however, really disliked him. Some of the oth-

ers liked him, and they all admired him for his courage.

Canty and Hugo did whatever they could to make the King miserable. The boy was still in Hugo's charge, and Hugo delighted in kicking him whenever the leader of the gang had his back turned.

One day, Hugo stepped on the King's

toes. He pretended that he had done it by accident. The King paid no attention to him and looked the other way. Hugo stepped on him again, and then again.

The King reached over and grabbed a staff from one of the outlaws nearby. He swung it in his arms and flattened Hugo with a single blow. The rest of the gang clapped their hands and cheered.

Hugo's face was red with anger. He sprang to his feet, grabbed a stick in his hands, and charged at the boy. But Hugo had little chance of winning. The King had been trained to fight with a staff by the best masters in England. He stood his ground and defended himself with ease against a rain of blows from Hugo. Once in a while, he moved in swiftly and rapped Hugo on the head.

Hugo was badly bruised. He turned and limped away from the field. The King was not harmed at all. He was swept up in a storm of cheers and paraded around on the men's shoulders.

Hugo was determined to have his

revenge on the King. All attempts to make the King beg or steal had failed. He would simply fold his arms on his chest and refuse to do anything that was against the law. Hugo decided he would take the King into a village. Then he, Hugo, would commit a crime and leave the King to take the blame for it. He wanted to have the King arrested and thrown into prison.

The next day, Hugo and the King were in a nearby village. The two drifted slowly up and down the streets. Hugo was watching for a chance to put his evil plan into effect. As usual, the King was watching for a chance to escape.

Hugo's chance came first. A woman came walking down the road with a big package in a basket on her arm. As the woman passed, Hugo slipped behind her and snatched the package out of her basket. Then he threw it into the King's hands and disappeared down a crooked alley.

The next moment, the woman realized her basket was empty and wheeled around to see Edward holding her package. She seized his wrist with one hand and snatched her bundle with the other shouting, "Thief! You stole my package!"

Hugo hid behind a post to watch the outcome of his trick. He saw that it was working, and he knew that the King would be taken prisoner by the law. He chuckled as he turned away, thinking of how sad he would pretend to be when he described "King Foo-Foo's" capture to the leader.

A crowd gathered around the King shaking their fists and shouting angry words. A strong blacksmith in a leather apron reached out to grab him, saying he would teach the boy a lesson. Just then, a long sword flashed in the air.

The sword stopped the blacksmith. Its owner said pleasantly, "Step back, please!"

The King cried happily, "Miles Hendon! I am truly glad to see you!"

An officer of the law arrived and led
Hendon, the King, and the screaming
woman with the package before a judge.
In the court, the woman pointed to
Edward and declared that he had stolen
her goods. The judge took the package
and unwrapped it. It contained a plump,
little pig. He looked up sternly.

"Good woman, how much is this pig
worth?"

"Forty pennies, your honor," she answered.

The judge said, "The law states that anyone who steals property worth more than thirteen pennies must hang!"

The woman gasped. The King's mouth dropped open in horror. Hendon's steady hand gripped the boy's shoulder.

"Your honor," pleaded Hendon, "please have mercy on this boy. I know

that he would never steal unless he had been forced to do so. If you will allow me, I will take care of him and see that he leads a good life."

The woman cried, "Oh your honor, I do not want this boy to die! Please let this good man take him. I will say my pig is worth only eight pennies in order to save him.

The judge stared at Edward. Finally, he said, "I will let him live, but he will have to go to prison."

The King started to cry out but Hendon said, "Your honor, please let me take the boy now. I am the son of a nobleman named Sir Richard Hendon. I will take him with me to my family's home in the country after I return to London."

The judge looked up in surprise. He looked at Hendon's threadbare clothes in puzzlement.

"If you are indeed Sir Richard's son..." he began.

"Please forgive my appearance," Hendon said quickly. "I have been away at war for more than seven years. But I can take care of the boy".

"All right, take him," the judge said.

Outside, Edward thanked Hendon and said, "You have saved me from injury and shame. For such special service to the crown I will make you my knight."

The King led Hendon over to a grassy

area behind the court where they could not be seen. He pointed to the ground before him. Miles Hendon, with a twinkle in his eye, dropped on one knee. Edward took Hendon's long sword in his own hand and touched him lightly on each shoulder with its flashing blade. Then he said,

"Rise, Sir Miles Hendon, Knight!"

Hendon thought to himself, "I am almost afraid to bring this poor child into London with me. What will he say when he learns that another boy will be crowned King of England there tomorrow?"

Chapter

The Royal Procession

While Edward, the true King, was wandering around the countryside with a band of beggars, Tom Canty was leading a splendid life in the palace—and beginning to enjoy it very much.

At first, Tom had been worried about the true Prince. Edward had been very kind to him and then suddenly disappeared after running off to punish the guard at the gate. As time wore on, though, and Edward still did not return, Tom had become more and more accustomed to the royal splendors around him.

Tom was also troubled by thoughts of his mother and sisters in the city. He

wanted to send for them and make them ladies. But he was sure the noblemen around him would ignore his orders, saying that his madness must have returned.

So, while the true King went hungry and thirsty—Tom marched to dinner attended by a glittering procession of noblemen.

While the true King wore rags and

shivered with cold—Tom enjoyed being dressed in robes of rich velvet. He slept on a bed of satin surrounded by an army of loyal servants, while the King wandered the city without a home.

The night before he was to be crowned King of England, Tom went to sleep a very happy boy.

The next morning, Tom was dressed

in the most splendid robes he had ever seen, and he rode on a beautiful, prancing horse. His noble adviser also mounted on a horse and took a place behind him. After them trailed what seemed like an endless parade of dazzling nobles and soldiers in shining armor.

Tom was to be crowned in a great church in the city of London. As he rode through the streets, thousands upon thousands of people shouted and cheered

to him. Their cries thundered through the air. Banners and flags waved on all sides.

Tom's heart swelled with pride. He caught sight of some of the ragged boys he had played with in the crowd.

"If only they knew whom they were really cheering," he thought, "how surprised they would all be!"

Tom smiled at them. He was about to raise his hand and wave to them when all of a sudden he saw another face he knew in the crowd. It was the pale, astonished face of his mother crying out to him. Tom gasped.

The next moment, his mother flew to his side crying, "Oh my child! My child!"

Tom was stunned. Before he could say or do anything, one of the royal guards charged over and hurled her back into the crowd. Tom turned away in horror. He couldn't bear to see his mother treated in such a way.

His eyes filled with tears. The cheering crowds blurred before him, and all he could see was the look of pain on his mother's face as she clung to his side. He was terribly ashamed to think that he had turned away from her. Suddenly, all his royal splendors meant nothing to him; they seemed as worthless as a pile of rotten rags.

The parade followed a winding, twisting course through the crooked lanes of the city. It looked like a giant serpent. Tom rode at the head of it with his face turned sadly downward.

Little by little, the cheering and

shouting stopped. The people were disappointed that their new King did not smile and wave to them. Tom's adviser rode up to him and said, "Your Majesty, please do not let the people see you looking so sad. Lift up your head and smile to them."

Tom tried to do as he was told. The procession moved slowly onward. With each step it took, it carried Tom Canty, the pauper, closer to the royal crown of England.

In the meantime, the *real* King

Edward had returned to London. He had become hopelessly separated from Miles Hendon in the crowds that followed the procession.

Now, Edward fought his way alone through a thick forest of moving arms and legs to the crown that was rightfully his.

Finally, as Tom Canty sat wrapped in a robe of golden cloth in front of the assembled noblemen and ladies of England, the end of the long ceremony was at hand. A deep hush spread through the great hall. All eyes were fixed on Tom Canty. The crown of England was held over his trembling head.

Suddenly, a ragged boy ran through the crowd. Edward had slipped into the church with the servants of the noblemen. He stopped halfway to the throne, raised his hand, and cried out in a clear voice, "I am the King!"

Fear and astonishment swept through the assembly. Everyone turned around and stared, wide-eyed, at the ragged boy. Many of the ladies started to scream, but then clasped their hands over their mouths.

Everywhere, hands flew up in surprise and then drifted slowly down. People were afraid to speak. The ancient ceremony of the crowning of the King, the most important occasion in history, had been stopped suddenly—by a pauper!

But what most amazed the people was not the fact that the ragged boy had stopped the ceremony, but the way he stood so boldly before them all. His feet seemed rooted to the ground. His clenched fists pressed against his hips. His head was high in the air. His courage was amazing!

Chapter

The Great Seal Mystery

Tom looked up and saw the enraged face of the true King challenging him to take the crown. And then, another face appeared in his mind. It was unclear at first. Then it became clearer. It was the face of his mother crying out to him.

Other faces appeared behind her, marching through his mind like a parade. He saw Nan, Bet, and Father Andrew, all tearful and sad. Then he saw the cruel face of the guard at the gate laughing at him, followed by the kind face of Edward questioning him about his life in the city.

Then came all the doubtful faces of the people who hadn't believed him and told him he was mad. What would happen if he tried to explain himself to Edward now? Would the true King believe him?

Or, would Edward call angrily for his royal guard and have him taken to prison? Tom looked up at his noble adviser. If he said nothing, he might be able to save his life . . . and remain King!

Tom's adviser was the first person to act. He had been appointed by Edward's father to protect the new King. He shouted. "Seize that beggar!"

The royal guards rushed forward and grabbed Edward. Tom knew exactly what he had to do. Without a second's delay, he ran to Edward.

"Take your hands off of him! He is the King!"

The noble adviser groaned, "The King is mad again."

Tom dropped on his knees before Edward.

"Oh Your Majesty," he cried, "put on the crown that is rightfully yours!"

The noble adviser looked very stern. He turned to face the ragged boy. Right away his sternness vanished. It was replaced by wonder.

"How strange!" he thought. "They look so alike!"

The noble adviser to the King found himself with a very serious problem. He had to decide which of the boys in front of him was the true King! The crowd began to murmur. Soon, everyone was whispering, "Which boy is the King of England?"

The noble adviser questioned Edward

about the court and the palace. He answered everything correctly, but still the adviser was not satisfied.

Suddenly, his face lit up. He had an idea.

"Can you tell me where the Great Seal of England is?" he asked. "It was given to the Prince of Wales to keep before he was troubled by madness, and it has not been seen since."

Edward said, "Take me to the palace and I will get it for you. It is in my private cabinet."

The advisor thought for a moment. He really had no choice but to take the two boys to the palace. He couldn't just have one thrown into prison. He called on his guards and led the boys to a carriage.

The group quickly made their way through the London streets, while back at the church, the crowd remained restless.

The King and Tom Canty began to feel at ease, thinking that their troubles would soon be over. They walked into the palace, smiling. Edward was glad to be home, and

Tom was thinking happily of returning to his poor mother and sisters.

The group made their way to the rooms of the former Prince. Edward went straight away for his cabinet and threw open its doors.

Much to his surprise, the cabinet was empty. Tom gasped and looked at Edward. What would they do now?

The advisor laughed cruelly. His face then became red with anger.

"Enough of this nonsense!" cried the

adviser. "Guards, seize that beggar and throw him in prison!"

"Wait!" cried Tom. "I know what you are talking about! Think, your Majesty, of what you did just before you ran out to punish the guard."

Edward thought and thought. The crown of England depended on his answer.

"I cannot tell you where it is," he said at last in a thin, weary voice. He was very, very pale.

"Think, Your Majesty!" cried Tom. "Think! You saw something lying on the table, didn't you?"

"Ah yes!" exclaimed Edward. "I saw the Great Seal on the table, snatched it up, and . . ."

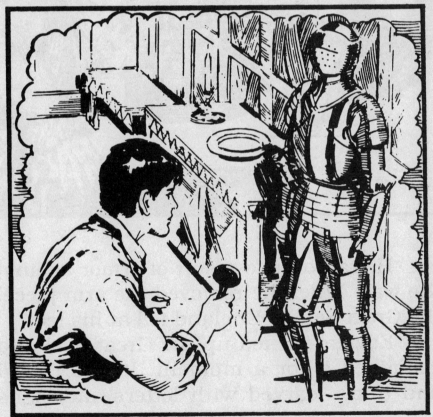

He ran over to a suit of armor against the wall. When he removed the arm piece, the Great Seal of England fell at his feet.

Edward picked up the Great Seal and examined it for a moment. It was round and thick—carved with letters and signs of English royalty. Edward gripped its strong handle with all his might. When the Great Seal was pressed into hot wax on a sheet of paper, it left a picture that could not be copied anywhere. It meant that the paper had come from the person who wore the royal crown of England!

The adviser shouted, "Long live the King."

The adviser turned and grabbed Tom angrily.

"I will throw this pretender into the Tower myself!" he said.

But Edward held up his hand and cried, "Stop! If it weren't for him, you would have thrown me into prison only a little while ago!"

Tom Canty fell on his knees and cried, "Oh my King! Now is the time for you to take back your royal garments and give me my poor pauper's rags!"

Edward smiled and said, "Now is the time for me to return to my people and be crowned!"

He took the robe of golden cloth from

Tom and put it on his shoulders. The robe hid his poor, tattered clothes from sight.

Quickly, they returned to the great church. The people were waiting for their true King!

In a matter of minutes, the ancient ceremony began again. The true King Edward was finally crowned. Outside, cannons boomed and cheers shook the city of London.

There was one thing about the loss of the Great Seal that bothered King Edward very much. He couldn't understand how Tom Canty could remember where he had put the Great Seal when he could not remember himself.

He decided that as soon as he had a moment, he would ask. Meanwhile he was glad that his pauper friend was so honest. If it had not been for Tom Canty's good character, the throne would have been taken over by a false king.

Chapter

A Happy Ending

The mystery of the Great Seal was solved some time later—after all the excitement of the crowning was over.

"Oh, your Majesty," said Tom, "it was easy for me to remember where the Seal was hidden because I took it out and used it many times."

"I don't understand," said the King. "What did you use it for?"

Tom blushed. He lowered his eyes and said, "Oh sir, I used it to crack nuts."

The King laughed heartily when he heard this.

But when Edward rode toward the palace after being crowned King, it was not the Great Seal that worried him. He thought of Hendon, and of how he must have been searching everywhere for him.

"He left the city to search for me after I was tricked into leaving his house," thought the King. "Surely he must be

looking for me now. I need to find him, but how? There must be a way."

Hendon had been tramping through the streets of London, pushed for hours by the crowds following the royal procession.

"Where can my little madman be?" he

thought. Hendon figured he would find the boy, as usual, in the middle of a crowd of people, shouting that he was the King.

Finally, he heard trumpets sounding. He knew that the royal procession was about to pass. He waited eagerly for a glimpse of the new King. At last Edward came riding by, and the sight of him in his royal robes almost took Hendon's breath away.

"Is it a dream?" He cried. "Is he truly the King, just as he has claimed?"

Hendon rushed forward and was seized by the guards that surrounded the King.

Edward called out, "Let him go! He is my loyal knight, Sir Miles Hendon! Bring him a horse this instant! He shall ride to the palace by my side!"

In the palace, the King brought Hendon before the court and announced: "Hear me, all of you! This is trusty Miles Hendon, who risked his life to protect me from harm! He saved my life and, there-

fore, he saved the crown of England! I have made him a knight! Now I will make him a great lord! He shall have gold, lands, and houses!"

"This is my poor beggar boy?" thought Hendon. "It's remarkable!"

Just then, there was a stir at the other end of the room. Tom Canty entered and knelt before the King. He had been dressed in a rather unusual, colorful way.

The King said, "I am very pleased with you, Tom Canty. You behaved very well

when you were in my place. Have you found your mother and sisters?"

"Yes, Your Majesty," Tom said happily.

"Good," said Edward. "They will be well cared for, but your father will be punished."

The King turned to face the court. He said, "Listen everyone. From this day forward, Tom Canty will reside at Christ's Church in the city. When I was poor and miserable, I was turned away by the boys of Christ's Church. But Tom will be taught there and, in time, he will become one of the directors of the school. He deserves to be treated with very special regard by all who meet him. He will always be known by his special costume. No one may copy it. And he shall always be called by the title of the King's Ward."

Tom Canty lived to be a very old and respected man. Wherever he went, his clothes served to remind people that he had once been royal. They would take off their hats and salute him with the words, "Make way for the King's Ward!"

THE END

ABOUT THE AUTHOR

SAMUEL LANGHORNE CLEMENS was born on November 30, 1835 in Florida, Missouri. Four years later his family moved to Hannibal, a town on the Mississippi River. Here, Clemens experienced life in a river town, which later helped him write many of his stories.

When Clemens was just twelve years old, his father died. So, he started working at a newspaper as a printer's helper to support his family. But at eighteen, Clemens left home to find adventure.

When he was twenty-two, Clemens worked on a steamboat on the Mississippi River, helping the pilot. Then he headed west and started working as a journalist. In this new career he called himself Mark Twain.

After moving back east, Mark Twain wrote many books, including *Tom Sawyer*, *The Prince and the Pauper*, and *Huckleberry Finn*. He was a very successful writer and was a popular speaker with audiences around the country. Today, he is still considered one of America's greatest authors.

The Young Collector's
Illustrated Classics

Adventures of Robin Hood
Black Beauty
Call of the Wild
Dracula
Frankenstein
Heidi
Little Women
Moby Dick
Oliver Twist
Peter Pan
The Prince and the Pauper
The Secret Garden
Swiss Family Robinson
Treasure Island
20,000 Leagues Under the Sea
White Fang